For Harvey

This edition produced for The Book People Ltd
Hall Wood Avenue, Haydock, St Helens WA11 9UL, by
LITTLE TIGER PRESS
An imprint of Magi Publications
1 The Coda Centre, 189 Munster Road, London SW6 6AW
First published in Great Britain 2001
2001 © Diane and Christyan Fox
Diane and Christyan Fox have asserted their rights to
be identified as the author and illustrator of this work
under the Copyright, Designs and Patents Act, 1988.
Printed in China · All rights reserved
ISBN 1 85430 789 4
1 3 5 7 9 10 8 6 4 2

Fireman
PiggyWiggy

Christyan and Diane Fox

TED SMART

Whenever I see a fire engine racing by, I dream of all the things that I would do if I were a fearless fireman...

RRRRIIINNGGG...

I would wear
a big yellow hat
and slide down
a shiny pole
on my way to
an emergency...

a big red fire engine and a screaming siren.

Maybe I would climb a tall ladder to rescue someone stuck in a very high place...

or save
someone
stuck down
a deep
dark hole.

blazing fires

powerful

hose.

But it's always that in a real

good to know emergency...